Some Dogs Do

for
David

First published 2003 by Walker Books Ltd
87 Vauxhall Walk, London SE11 5HJ

This edition including DVD published 2007

10 9 8 7 6 5 4 3 2 1

© 2003 Jez Alborough

The right of Jez Alborough to be identified as author/illustrator
of this work has been asserted by him in accordance with the
Copyright, Designs and Patents Act 1988

This book has been typeset in Providence Sans Bold Educational

Printed in China

British Library Cataloguing in Publication Data:
a catalogue record for this book is available from the British Library

ISBN 978-1-4063-0831-0

www.walkerbooks.co.uk

Some Dogs Do

Jez Alborough

WALKER BOOKS
AND SUBSIDIARIES
LONDON · BOSTON · SYDNEY · AUCKLAND

When Sid set off for school one day,

a happy feeling came his way.

It filled him up so much he found

his paws just lifted off the ground.

Without a how,
without a why,

Sid fell up
towards the sky.

Through swirling puffs of cloud he twirled above a tiny toy-town world,

in the land
of sun and moon,

like a doggy-shaped
balloon.

At school Sid asked his best friend Ben,
"Did you see me fly just then?"

"Don't be daft," came Ben's reply.
"You're a dog, and *dogs don't fly.*"

"But *I did,*" said Sid.
"*I did ... I did.*"

In the classroom
Sid said, "Hey! Guess what!
I flew to school today!"

His classmates giggled, yelped and yowled.
"Dogs don't fly to school!" they howled.
"But *I did*," said Sid. "*I did.*"

Miss Mare the teacher shook her head.
"Now Sid, you shouldn't lie," she said.

"All dogs walk and jump and run,
    but *dogs don't fly* — it can't be done."

"But I did," said Sid.

Gus said, "Right! If you can fly, come outside ... let's see you try!"

Sid's happiness had gone by then.
He tried to get it back again.

He thought about   the clouds up high

and then he jumped towards the sky.

"You see, you're just a dog," said Gus,
"with paws for walking just like us.

That will teach you not to lie.
Now you know that *dogs don't fly*."

When Sid walked home from school that day,

it seemed a long and lonely way.

And once at home with Mum and Dad,
deep inside he still felt bad.

He did the things he always did,
but something wasn't right with Sid.

His dad came out and asked, "What's up?
You seem unhappy, little pup."

Sid sat staring at the sky,
and all he said was, "Dogs don't fly."

Sid's dad slowly raised his head.
"I know a secret, Sid," he said.
"Could you keep it safe inside?"

"What's the secret?"
Sid replied.

He turned around
and then ...
he knew...

Now you know

the secret too!

Sid's happy eyes were open wide.

"I knew it ... DOGS DO FLY!" he cried.

Sid's dad said, "Come, fly then, Sid,"

and that's exactly what Sid did.

Do dogs fly? Is it true?

Some dogs don't, and some dogs do.